_____

_____

_____

_____

_____

_____

_____

_____

◆　　◆　　◆

Published by Barbour Publishing, Inc., P.O. Box 719, Uhrichsville, Ohio 44683, www.barbourbooks.com

Our mission is to publish and distribute inspirational products offering exceptional value and biblical encouragement to the masses.

Member of the
Evangelical Christian
Publishers Association

Printed in China.
5 4 3 2

come to the MANGER

MARILOU H. FLINKMAN

DayMaker
GREETINGS

If holidays bring out visions of Santa Claus,

twinkling lights,

and reindeer with red noses,

you need to change your view.

Think Holy-days

and remember the first Christmas.

It all started with a manger.

I invite you to join me as we follow the path to the manger.

Let's start by going back to the prophets of old.

They will tell us where to start our journey.

◆　◆　◆

For unto us a child is born, unto us a son is given:

and the government shall be upon his shoulder:

and his name shall be called

Wonderful, Counsellor,
The mighty God,
The everlasting Father,
The Prince of Peace.

ISAIAH 9:6

Those ancient words bring hope to the world. How would we react if we saw those words as the headline in the morning paper? Would we scoff or would we fall on our knees in Thanksgiving?

Would we turn to the rest of the story on the back pages to see where this miracle man could be found? Or would we use the paper to line the birdcage?

Read Isaiah's words again and decide if you will set your course for the North Pole or join me to search for the Prince of Peace.

Together we can follow the path to find this
wonderful counselor, this mighty God who
will shoulder the government.
We won't find Him in a palace nor will He be in a big
government office. We will find the everlasting Father
in a manger. Come, let us search for that manger.

And it shall be said in that day,

Lo, this is our God;

we have waited for him,

and he will save us: this is the LORD;

we have waited for him,

we will be glad and rejoice in his salvation.

ISAIAH 25:9

He has come to save mankind. But in this world of wars, famine, and strife, where will we find Him? Isaiah's words are centuries old. Are we too late to find the Savior? Has He come and found us too sinful to save?

We are told to come to the manger. Where will we find this place? Will it be the same for all of us? Follow the prophets for a clue to the answers.

But thou, Bethlehem Ephratah, though thou

be little among the thousands of Judah,

yet out of thee shall he come forth unto me

that is to be ruler in Israel;

whose goings forth have been from of old, from everlasting.

MICAH 5:2

Come Thou long expected Jesus,

Born to set Thy people free;

From our fears and sins release us;

Let us find our rest in Thee.

Israel's strength and consolation,

Hope of all the earth Thou art;

Dear desire of every nation,

Joy of every longing heart.

Born Thy people to deliver,

Born a child, and yet a King,

Born to reign in us for ever,

Now Thy gracious kingdom bring.

By Thine own eternal Spirit,

Rule in all our hearts alone;

By Thine all-sufficient merit,

Raise us to Thy glorious throne.

OLD ENGLISH HYMN

And in the sixth month the angel

Gabriel was sent from God

unto a city of Galilee, named Nazareth. . . .

And the angel said unto her, Fear not, Mary:

for thou hast found favour with God.

And, behold, thou shalt conceive in thy womb,

and bring forth a son, and shalt call his name

Jesus.

He shall be great, and shall be called

the Son of the Highest:

and the Lord God shall give unto him

the throne of his father David:

And he shall reign over the house of Jacob for ever;

and of his kingdom there shall be no end.

LUKE 1:26, 30–33

The young teen Mary listened to the angel who explained how these things would be possible. The daily routine of her life would be turned upside down and thrown into confusion. Yet with great faith she faced the unknown and said, "Yes."

And Mary said,

Behold the handmaid of the Lord;

be it unto me according to thy word.

And the angel departed from her.

LUKE 1:38

Then Joseph her husband,

being a just man,

and not willing to make her a public example,

was minded to put her away privily.

But while he thought on these things,

behold, the angel of the LORD appeared

unto him in a dream, saying,

Joseph, thou son of David,

fear not to take unto thee Mary thy wife:

for that which is conceived in her is of the Holy Ghost.

And she shall bring forth a son,

and thou shalt call his name JESUS:

for he shall save his people from their sins.

MATTHEW 1:19–21

Joseph expected life to take a predictable course—a wedding, a family, and the daily life of a carpenter. When Mary came to him with her story, he was ready to quietly bow out. Then an angel came to him with the message that overcame human logic. Could this be true? Could this young girl to whom he was betrothed actually bring forth the Son of God?

The beauty of Mary and Joseph's faith sets the example for us. We must continue on the path to find a world of peace. We must seek justice and love. We must seek the Christ Child.

And Mary arose in those days,

and went into the hill country with haste,

into a city of Juda;

And entered into the house of Zacharias,

and saluted Elisabeth.

And it came to pass, that,

when Elisabeth heard the salutation of Mary,

the babe leaped in her womb;

and Elisabeth was filled with the Holy Ghost:

And she spake out with a loud voice, and said,

Blessed art thou among women,

and blessed is the fruit of thy womb.

And whence is this to me,

that the mother of my Lord should come to me

LUKE 1:39–43

Can't you see a young confused girl running to a favorite relative to be consoled? When Mary came to her cousin and Elisabeth greeted her with joy, she must have felt comfort. Elisabeth recognized Mary's condition and the details of how it came to be. Mary could relax in the knowledge that Elisabeth, whom she loved and trusted, understood her story.

And Mary abode with her about three months,
and returned to her own house.

LUKE 1:56

Mary

had to return to the world she grew up in. Nazareth must have buzzed with gossip. The quick trip to visit her cousin and sudden marriage to Joseph would have set tongues wagging. But we have seen the strength of this young woman.

She is no ordinary bride.

She is preparing herself to care
for the Son of God.
She is following the path
God has set before her.

And it came to pass in those days,
that there went out a decree from Caesar Augustus
that all the world should be taxed. (And this taxing
was first made when Cyrenius was governor of
Syria.) And all went to be taxed,
every one into his own city.

LUKE 2:1–3

God even uses the taxman!
The Christ Child was to be born in Bethlehem,
and this is how the Lord brought Mary to the place
spoken of in the prophets.

And Joseph also went up from Galilee,

out of the city of Nazareth,

into Judaea, unto the city of David,

which is called Bethlehem;

(because he was of the house and lineage of David:)

to be taxed with Mary his espoused wife,

being great with child.

LUKE 2:4–5

◆　◆　◆

Nine months pregnant and riding a donkey from

Nazareth to Bethlehem shows this girl's courage.

Could our path be any harder?

Can we stop now on our goal to find the manger?

And so it was, that, while they were there,
the days were accomplished that she should be delivered.
And she brought forth her firstborn son,
and wrapped him in swaddling clothes,
and laid him in a manger;

because there was no room for them in the inn.

LUKE 2:6–7

◆ ◆ ◆

There was no sterile hospital, not even a midwife.

The Son of God was born in a stable.

His humble bed a manger, the very manger we seek today.

How will we find our way? Faith will be our guide.

And there were in the same country shepherds abiding in the field, keeping watch over their flock by night. And, lo, the angel of the Lord came upon them, and the glory of the Lord shone round about them: and they were sore afraid.

And the angel said unto them, Fear not: for, behold, I bring you good tidings of great joy, which shall be to all people.

For unto you is born this day in the city of David a Saviour, which is Christ the Lord.

And this shall be a sign unto you; Ye shall find the babe wrapped in swaddling clothes, lying in a manger.

And suddenly there was with the angel a multitude of the heavenly host praising God, and saying,

Glory to God in the highest, and on earth peace, good will toward men.

Luke 2:8–14

The first to worship at the manger were shepherds from the fields. The angels of heaven guided them to the Christ Child. These were simple workingmen who probably could not read. We have the prophets of old and the Scriptures of the Gospels to guide us. They followed the star of Bethlehem to the stable. We will follow the light that still shines in the world if we will but look for it.

Don't be led astray by the tinsel and flickering lights of the secular world around us. Seek the radiance of God's glory. We can only miss it if we aren't looking.

And it came to pass,

as the angels were gone away from them into heaven,

the shepherds said one to another,

Let us now go even unto Bethlehem,

and see this thing which is come to pass,

which the Lord hath made known unto us.

And they came with haste, and found Mary, and Joseph,

and the babe lying in a manger.

And when they had seen it, they made known abroad

the saying which was told them concerning this child.

And all they that heard it wondered at those things

which were told them by the shepherds.

LUKE 2:15–18

Who is this child in the manger?
Could it be the Son of God would come into

the world not only as a newborn baby

but consent to be born in a barn?

He lies wrapped in strips of cloth

His mother brought with her.

The star over the stable still shines,

but the angels are gone. Humble shepherds kneel

by the manger in awe of what they see there.

Now when Jesus was born in Bethlehem of Judaea in the days of Herod the king, behold,

there came wise men from the east to Jerusalem, saying,
Where is he that is born King of the Jews? for we have seen
his star in the east, and are come to worship him.

MATTHEW 2:1–2

◆ ◆ ◆

The wise men followed the star and found Jesus.
They fell on their knees and worshiped
the Christ Child. They gave Him gifts of gold,
frankincense, and myrrh.

And being

warned of God

in a dream

that they should not return to Herod,

they departed into their own country

another way.

MATTHEW 2:12

Will we be like these wise men of old? Will we jump out of the rat race to celebrate Christmas with prayer and gifts to others? When the glitter of the celebration is past, will we follow the words of Christ and go on with life on the Christian path?

The wise men turned away from the evil they saw in Herod. Let's take a lesson from them and avoid the lure of the world. Let's look for the manger and the blessing waiting there for us.

And when eight days were accomplished for the circumcising of the child, *his name was called Jesus,* which was so named of the angel before he was conceived in the womb. And when the days of her purification according to the law of Moses were accomplished, they brought him to Jerusalem, to present him to the LORD.

LUKE 2:21–22

Joseph and Mary

obeyed the laws of Moses.

They brought the baby for circumcision

and called His name *Jesus*.

The name was not uncommon,

being a later form of the Hebrew name Joshua,

meaning savior.

And, behold,

there was a man in Jerusalem, whose name was Simeon;

and the same man was just and devout,

waiting for the consolation of Israel:

and the Holy Ghost was upon him.

And it was revealed unto him by the Holy Ghost, that he

should not see death, before he had seen the Lord's Christ.

And he came by the Spirit into the temple: and when the

parents brought in the child Jesus, to do for him

after the custom of the law, then took he him up in his arms,

and blessed God, and said, Lord, now lettest thou

thy servant depart in peace, according to thy word:

For mine eyes have seen thy salvation,

which thou hast prepared before the face of all people;

a light to lighten the Gentiles,

and the glory of thy people Israel.

LUKE 2:25–32

Led by the Holy Spirit, Simeon waited in the temple when Jesus was presented by His parents. We will be led to the manger where Christ waits if we are just willing to follow the Spirit.

◆ ◆ ◆

Anna and Simeon were called into the temple to receive the Christ Child. Where will we be?

We have followed the path.
Our manger is waiting.
Whether it is in a church, the company of laughing children

and loved ones, or in the silence of a hospital room,

or a lonely apartment. You only have to close your eyes

and open your heart and

come to the manger.

Jesus Christ is waiting for you.

Glory to God
in the highest,
and peace to
His people
on earth.